THE ADVENTURES OF

AMAZING GRACE

ERIKA FERRARI LOPEZ

 MARIPOSA LIT

Erika Ferrari Lopez is an independent author of children's fiction aged 8+.
erikaferrarilopezauthor@gmail.com
Web: www.erikaferrarilopez.com

Cover and interior art by Amber Orozco
Cover hand lettering by Sol Herrera
Book design and typesetting by Sheila Smallwood

ISBN 979-8-9884790-0-0
Library of Congress Catalog Number has been applied for.

Mariposa Lit
Charlotte, NC

To my Mami, who taught me to fly,
and my daughter, Sophia, who
gave me wings.

keep soaring!

♡Erika

"'Twas grace that taught my heart to fear
And grace my fears relieved
How precious did that grace appear
The hour I first believed"

"Amazing Grace"

CONTENTS

1
The Secret

At the end of the summer when Grace turned nine, she realized something big. While jumping on her trampoline, Grace discovered she could slow down her jumps. Well, not on the way up. That was normal.

She would crouch down, then leap, extending her long legs, and get so very high. But on the way down she could actually slow her fall before her feet hit the trampoline again. Floating for a second or two before she touched down, it was almost as if … she could fly!

But that's just not possible, right? Grace thought.

Not sure what was happening, Grace continued experimenting in the privacy of her bedroom. While her dad was at the office, her mom worked downstairs, and her big brother, Gabriel, was busy doing whatever it was he did in the basement, she'd spend most of the day jumping off her bed.

Grace kept pushing herself to see just how high and how far she could go. Thankfully, she had a fluffy white shag rug in her room because she had more than a few falls. But after two weeks, she had learned how to jump off the bed, hover a few inches above the ground, and come down on one foot, light as a feather.

Once she could hover, Grace focused on jumping just a little bit further, a few more inches every day until she was crossing her entire room without touching the ground once. She didn't know what to make of this new skill, so she kept it a secret.

She didn't even tell her parents. I mean, what do you say? "Mom, Dad, I can fly!" That sounded CRAZY!

And who knew, this thing, whatever it was, could go away tomorrow. Besides, Gabriel didn't need one more reason to tease her. Since he had started middle school last year, it seemed like the only time her big brother talked to her was to point out how lame she was. No, for now, she'd just keep this to herself.

Soon enough, it was time to go back to school. Grace was bursting to share what she had learned that summer with her best friend, Adrian, who had been away at theater camp for two whole weeks. But she wasn't quite sure if she could tell him either. She decided to keep it a secret, at least for now.

Grace was thrilled she and Adrian were in the same class again, and third grade started just like any other school year, except, that is, for Grace's secret.

Grace was careful not to fly at school. Well, until she discovered that she LOVED practicing her flying in the school gymnasium.

Grace knew it was risky, but there was so much space—no dressers or lamps she could bump into like in her room. No, in the gym it was all wide open, and she had figured out how to make sure no one could watch her.

Once PE class was over, her homeroom teacher, Mrs. Rings, would line everyone up to go back to their classroom. That's when Grace would pretend to tie her shoe or forget her water bottle until everyone was moving down the hallway. Double checking that the PE teacher had gone into her office, Grace would leap as far as she could.

By the end of September, she could jump from the free throw line to the end of the court without touching the ground!

No one guessed what she was up to, until one day after PE, Adrian turned around from his spot at the end of the line while Grace was mid-flight in the gym. His jaw dropped, and while the rest of the class walked down the hall to their classroom, he stood there, frozen.

Grace panicked and dropped to the ground. Panting, she ran to where he stood. Adrian slowly closed his mouth and swallowed hard.

"Did I just see what I think I saw?"

Grace didn't know what to say. Should

she tell him? What would he think? She didn't say a thing, just rushed past him to catch up with the rest of the class, leaving him glued to the spot.

Once Mrs. Rings settled the class into their math lesson, a folded note flew from behind Grace and landed on her desk. Unfolding it carefully, Grace read Adrian's handwriting.

"Can you really fly? Check ___ Yes ___ No" She folded the note quickly and looked around to make sure no one had seen it. Then she shoved it in her pocket and tried to focus on her math worksheet.

For the rest of the afternoon, she never looked up, even though she could feel Adrian's eyes on her back. When the bell rang at the end of the school day, Grace rushed to get her bookbag at the back of the classroom.

Before Adrian could catch up to her,

she got into the walkers line and filed out of the classroom and the school. Her mom was waiting with her usual group of mom friends on the blacktop.

"Hi, honey! How was your day?" her mom asked.

Grace ran into her mom's arms and didn't let go.

"Oof, it was a doozy, huh? Why don't we skip the playground today and head home for a snack?" her mom suggested.

Grace nodded and grabbed her mom's hand. She didn't let go for the three-block walk to their house.

2
Antepasados

 **Ancestors**

Bitter tea popular in South America

Grace settled at the kitchen island while her mom boiled water for their **yerba mate** tea. Grace's dad was from Argentina, and the whole family loved this bitter tea he had grown up drinking, sweetened with a lot of sugar, of course. Grace's favorite part was drinking it out of her own special gourd cup with a metal straw, just like her dad's family had done in Argentina.

Grace's mom poured the hot water over the mate leaves in her cup, and Grace waited for the tea to steep. Taking a nibble of a crunchy **empanada**, Grace already felt better.

Baked or fried dough filled with meat, vegetables, or fruit

"Grace, has something been bothering you lately?" her mom asked. "I noticed you spent a lot of time upstairs alone this summer and now after school. You seem upset this afternoon. What's going on?"

Grace wasn't sure whether she should tell her mom her secret. She was worried her mom would be upset or think she was weird or wrong in some way. But Adrian had seen her in the gym, so her secret was out. The memory of Adrian's stare and the folded note in her pocket weighed on her. Grace took a deep breath and said, "Mom, there's something I have to show you."

Grace got up from the kitchen island and leapt. When she touched down on the other side of the kitchen, much further than she could have gone with any normal jump, she looked at her mom.

To Grace's surprise, her mom had a big smile on her face.

She responded, "Watch this," and then leapt, right from her spot in front of the stove, high, high up in the air, much higher than Grace had ever gone. She touched down softly on the other side of the kitchen island.

"Mom!" Grace yelled, running to wrap her arms around her mother's waist. Her mom reached down and squeezed Grace tight. "You can fly?" Grace asked.

"Yes, honey," her mom responded, "and I'm so happy to see that you can too." Grace had so many questions.

"Does Dad know?"

"Yes."

"Can he fly, too?"

"No."

"Can Gabriel?"

"No."

"Who else?"

"Your **abuela** and every female ancestor on my mother's side that we know of."

Grand-mother

And of course, Grace's biggest question, "How?"

"Let's sit down," her mother said, and after Grace had settled back down at the kitchen island, she began her story.

"Many generations ago, one of our ancestors was working in a field in **Guatemala.** She had tied her baby girl onto her back in a **mochila,** when she heard the grass crunching behind her. She turned to find a crouching jaguar eyeing her and her baby.

Country in Central America, south of Mexico

Knapsack or back-pack

Without a moment to think, she grabbed her baby out of her pack. Spotting a large nest on a low branch, she tossed the bundled baby into a nearby tree. She swung around to face the animal. With wild waves, jabs, and yelps, the mother successfully scared the jaguar back into the jungle.

The mother turned back to her baby just in time to see her topple out of the nest. She screamed a prayer, **'¡Dios mío! Ayúdala,'** and watched in horror, and then awe, as the baby dropped from the tree only to stop inches above the rocky ground. The bundle had hovered for a second, then touched down slowly, light as a feather, without a scratch.

My God!
Help her!

Since then, each of the female descendants have found that they could hover above the earth. And with practice, fly."

With wide eyes, Grace took a large sip of the mate tea.

"Why not the boys?" she asked. No one knew. The male relatives and husbands, like Grace's dad, had become guardians of the secret, but could not fly.

"Is Gabriel a guardian?" Grace asked.

"Not yet. He hasn't had anyone to help protect … until now. He doesn't know about any of this. We'll share this with him when the time is right so he can start training with Dad."

Grace nodded, relieved that she didn't have to tell her brother right away.

"Will you help me get better?" Grace asked.

"Of course, **m'hija,**" her mother responded with a big hug. "We'll practice together. But this is our family secret. It's important you don't tell anyone else about this or let anyone see you fly."

My daughter

Grace gulped and nodded.

🦋 🦋 🦋

That night, after Gabriel went down to the basement to play video games and her dad cleaned up the dishes from dinner, Grace stayed up well past her bedtime working on new flying skills with her mom in their secluded backyard.

Grace's mom explained that it was important to rise and fall with control.

"It looks like you've learned how to jump and hover already. So to go up or down, you use your legs to climb. It's like you're on imaginary stairs."

Grace watched as her mom lifted off the ground by moving her legs up one at a time until she was way over Grace's head.

"Use your arms to help control your speed or stop. If you need to slow down, hold your arms out, and if you need to stop, put your hands out in front of you like stop signs."

Grace watched her mom's graceful arm movements and copied them from the ground. Now it was her turn to try.

Grace jumped and hovered in the air.

Then she started moving her legs. She couldn't believe how easy it was to rise this way. But when she looked down and saw how high she was off the ground, she panicked.

Putting her hands out to stop and hover, she called down, "Mom, what do I do to get down? I'm going to fall!"

Her mom called up, "Calm your breathing. You're doing great. Just start climbing down imaginary stairs to get back down."

Grace climbed back down and ran into her mom's arms.

"You're amazing, Grace! A natural!" Her mom squeezed her tight.

When they were done practicing, Grace was able to fly as high as the top of their one-story house! The two of them flew up to the roof of their back porch and sat gazing at the moon. It was amazing to be so high up, with her mom next to her. They spotted an owl with huge eyes in a nearby tree that seemed surprised to see them at eye level.

Leaning against her mom's arm, Grace thought about Adrian. But she didn't want to ruin the moment by telling her mom that he had caught her flying. Tired and happy, she decided she'd tell her mom about it on the walk to school tomorrow morning.

3
Seen!

The next day at school drop off, Grace gave her mom an extra-long hug, happy to have finally shared her flying secret with her. Grace bounded up the path to the school entrance when she remembered she hadn't told her mom about Adrian!

As her mom walked away, Grace called out, "Mom!"

"Yes?" her mom replied. But by then

teachers were herding the kids into the school, and Grace was being pushed along by the crowd. She couldn't say any more.

"Never mind," Grace called back miserably. She'd have to tell her mom after school.

All morning Grace felt Adrian's eyes on the back of her head from his seat two rows back. She kept her eyes glued to her paper, looking up only if her teacher was talking or to glance at the clock. It was already 11:00 a.m. Lunchtime was coming!

She and Adrian always sat together at lunch. There was no way to avoid him. Should she admit to him that she could fly? Her mom had said to keep it a family secret.

But Grace thought, *I mean, Adrian is like family, and he already saw me.*

🦋 🦋 🦋

"Sooooo … " Adrian slid in next to Grace at the cafeteria table. "Are you going to tell me if I saw what I think I saw yesterday? I couldn't sleep a wink last night trying to figure it out." He lowered his voice and glanced side to side to make sure no one was listening. "Can you really…fly?"

After slowly tearing all the crust off her sandwich, Grace was out of stalling tactics. She took a deep breath.

"Shhhh…don't say it so loud. But… yes," she whispered.

"WOOOOHOOO!" Adrian yelped. Grace's cheeks flushed.

"QUIET! You can't tell anyone!" she said in a harsh whisper.

Grace quickly looked around. Across the cafeteria Mrs. Rings put her finger to her mouth to signal for them to be quiet, then returned to her conversation with another teacher.

Adrian didn't seem to hear Grace's scolding. He was smiling ear to ear. Grace had to mirror his big grin. She started giggling, and so did he. Before they knew it, they were doubled over, laughing so hard they couldn't make a sound.

Once they finally caught their breath, Adrian was full of questions. Grace tried to answer what she could, but she realized she didn't know that much about how it worked.

"At first, I could kind of hover when I jumped on the trampoline. And then I started experimenting in my room. I gave myself goals to get from my bed to the bookcase, then to the end of the rug, and then to the door. It's taken a while, but I can get from the free throw line to the basket in the gym now without touching the floor. And last night my mom taught me how to go high! We even sat on our roof!"

"Whoa!" Adrian shook his head, still smiling. **"¿Enséñame?"**

Show me

Grace thought back to all the things she and Adrian had taught each other. They had known each other since preschool. It was a bilingual preschool and Grace had come in knowing more Spanish, while Adrian had spoken only English. They had been matched up at the same table to learn from each other. To this day they still used Spanish when there just wasn't the right English word.

Their friendship and learning had continued to elementary school. When Adrian had taken tap dance lessons in first grade, he had taught Grace all the steps. And when Grace joined the soccer team, she had recreated the practice drills for Adrian in her yard. But Adrian was no athlete.

Grace didn't think she could pass on

the gift of flying to her friend. But looking at Adrian's eager face, she shrugged her shoulders and said, **"¿Puedo tratar?"**

I can try

At recess, they ran to the side of the schoolyard no one used. Most of the kids played kickball or tag on the blacktop. Everyone else would be on the swings or monkey bars. So the small field next to the school was empty and out of sight thanks to some overgrown bushes.

Grace found two sticks and placed them on the ground a little further apart than regular jumping distance.

"Let's try hovering first," she said. He stood at one stick, bent his knees, and jumped with all his might. But he didn't make it close to the second stick.

"OK, so what do I do?" he asked.

Flying

"Well, you kind of picture yourself floating, **volando,** right above the ground and keep your feet up and moving," Grace explained.

"Sounds easy enough." Adrian went back to his starting stick, bent his legs, scrunched up his face, leapt, pedaled his feet…and landed in the same spot as the first time. "Show me how you do it," he said.

"Well, OK."

Looking around to make sure no one was watching, Grace put her feet at the starting stick and leapt. Moving her feet like she was walking slowly in mid-air, her body hovered above the ground until she landed softly on her right foot, well past the second stick.

"So cool!" Adrian shouted.

Just then, Grace turned around and saw the art teacher, Mrs. Lavin, in the window of the second-floor stairwell of the school. She was looking right at them, hands on her head, astonished eyes blinking hard through her thick glasses.

4
Mrs. Lavin's Visit

Fast! "¡**Rápido!**" Grace shouted at Adrian.

She tore off in the direction of the playground. *Maybe if we blend in with the kids on the slides and monkey bars, Mrs. Lavin won't be able to pick us out of the crowd,* Grace thought.

But Adrian was still glued to the spot where Grace had left him. He faced Mrs.

Lavin from field to window, their eyes locked. He was never good in a high-pressure situation.

The bell rang and everyone ran to line up. The bell must have broken Adrian and Mrs. Lavin's gaze because he sprinted from the grassy field to the end of the line. Grace, in the middle of the line, made sure she didn't catch his or anyone else's eye as they shuffled single file back into the school.

Grace's mind raced. *From that distance could Mrs. Lavin know for sure she had seen someone flying? Could she pick out that it was me?*

Back in their classroom, Mrs. Rings announced Drop Everything and Read time, and everyone got out their books of choice. Grace snuggled into a low beanbag by the sunny window, the furthest spot from the door.

Taking deep breaths, Grace got her

heartbeat to slow down. She was trying hard to focus on her book when she heard footsteps coming into the room. Sure enough, it was Mrs. Lavin and she started urgently whispering to Mrs. Rings.

Grace sunk as far as she could into her beanbag, holding her book over her face. But her stomach turned a backflip when she heard Mrs. Rings call out, "Adrian?"

Grace peered over her book. Adrian rose from the corner he'd been huddled into, dropping his book on his desk as he passed it. He walked slowly toward the two teachers. Grace strained to hear their conversation but only caught the words "playground" and "follow me" as Adrian left the room with Mrs. Lavin. Grace caught his eye just before he disappeared out the door and out of sight.

Grace's heart raced again. *What had Mrs. Lavin seen exactly? Why hadn't she asked for me too? Maybe she didn't recognize me. That's good. Right?* Her biggest worry now was would Adrian tell.

"Whoa! What did Adrian do? He's in trouble!" Nolton called out.

Nolton had also been in the same class with Grace and Adrian since kindergarten but had always been jealous of their friendship. Smart in class, but downright mean at times on the playground, especially to Adrian, Nolton always managed to draw the spotlight to himself.

Mrs. Rings told Nolton to get back to his book, but he swung around and narrowed his dark eyes at Grace.

"I bet you had something to do with this," he mouthed.

Grace's face flushed with anger, and she tried to focus on her book while she waited for her friend to return. But the words kept moving around on the page as she imagined the awful things that would happen if Mrs. Lavin knew about her flying.

It felt as though ants were crawling all over her skin as she waited for Adrian to come back to class. When he finally did, just before dismissal, he looked miserable as he shuffled back to his seat. While everyone packed their backpacks, Grace turned full around in her chair and cleared her throat loudly.

With raised eyebrows she mouthed, "What happened?" Adrian didn't answer, he just shook his head and got up to get his backpack from the back hooks.

Grace followed him. Just then the loudspeaker came to life with the afternoon announcements, masking the sound of Nolton sneaking up behind her.

"You better tell me what's going on. You know I'm going to find out what happened!" But Adrian's name was first to be called for carpool, and Grace had to join the walkers line to the blacktop.

"I'm going to find out!" Nolton called to them both as they hurried out of the classroom in separate directions.

Grace was so scared that her family's secret, a secret guarded for generations, had been spilled in one afternoon—and it was all her fault.

5
Behind the Wall

Grace's mom was waiting outside the school as usual. Grace broke into a run. "I need to talk to you," she said as soon as she reached her.

"Are you OK, honey?" Her mom searched her face for clues.

"Yes, but we need to go, like, now!"

Grace's mom gave a quick wave to the

other parents and put her arm around Grace.

As they walked home, she asked, "What happened, **mi amor?**"

My love

Grace waited until they were well past the school before answering. Taking a deep breath, she spilled it all out.

"She saw me! I didn't tell you that Adrian saw me yesterday, and today I was showing him how I could fly at recess, and…Mrs. Lavin saw me!"

Grace covered her face with her hands, and the tears came quickly. Her mom grabbed Grace's hands and looked into her eyes.

"Grace, when did this happen? You have to remember exactly. What time was it?"

Grace saw urgency in her mom's expression. *Time? Didn't she care that Mrs. Lavin had seen? That Adrian knew?*

"I guess, I mean, the bell at the end of

recess rings at 12:30. It was a few minutes before that, so 12:26, 12:27?"

Her mother exhaled and started walking more quickly than normal. She pulled her phone out of her back pocket and called Grace's dad.

I love you

"Hey. She's been seen. Can you get back? OK. See you at home. **Te amo.**"

By the time they walked up to the house, Grace's dad was pulling into the driveway. He leapt out of the car and hurried towards them.

"Are you OK?" he asked Grace.

"Yes, I'm sorry. One day after learning about all this and I've already ruined the secret."

Relax

"Tranquila. It's happened before. We can fix this," her dad said, wrapping his arm around her shoulder

Fix this? Grace wondered. *But how? Why was dad home?*

They went down to the basement, and

her dad led them into the storage room. *Where are we going?* Grace wondered.

He walked right up to a cement wall and with a light push it opened. It was a door! It noiselessly swung in on hidden hinges, and Grace peered inside.

What is this place? Grace wondered.

"This is your dad's time lab," her mother said, as if reading Grace's mind. "It's where Dad helps me whenever someone has seen my magic. He'll help you too, honey."

There were clocks everywhere—on every surface, with labels for different countries and time zones. There were also ones marked with labels like *"Violet 2009"* and *"Abuela 1978."* There were big clocks and small ones. There were clocks that looked like antiques and more modern-looking clocks, but they were all analog, the kind with hands. The room had to be soundproof because the ticking of the clocks was almost deafening, but Grace had never heard anything in the basement. "You know what we need to do," her father said, looking at Grace's mother.

"We'll double back to the school. You stay here and start preparing. Gabriel's bus will be here soon," she said. "You should probably fill him in. We're going to need more guardians." Grace's mom helped clear off the large table in the center of the room.

Grace's dad pulled out a machine that looked like a giant antique hourglass except for the dials, cranks, and etchings all over the sides. He put it on the tall table at eye level for Grace. She was just about to touch one of the beautifully carved knobs on the side of the machine when her mother grabbed her hand and announced that they needed to go back to the school.

"What for?" Grace asked.

"To get a clock from where Mrs. Lavin was standing when she saw you."

6
Back to School

Grace blinked, not believing what was happening. But knowing all of this was her fault for flying at school, she followed her mother out of the room and back upstairs. Grace thought about what her mom just told her.

"A clock?" she said. "I don't know if there's a clock in that hallway. Wait. There is! I've seen it at the very top of the stairwell. Way high up."

"OK, that's good, much easier than getting hold of Mrs. Lavin's watch. We're taking the car." Her mom grabbed her keys. *Wow,* Grace thought, *we must really be in a hurry.*

As they drove, Grace was full of questions. "Why do we need a clock? What will happen to Mrs. Lavin?"

"Your father can't reverse time. Only bend it," her mom said. She drove quickly down the street.

"Bend it? What does that mean?" Grace couldn't believe what her mom was saying. "He'll slow down the exact moment when Mrs. Lavin looked out the window so much that she'll assume she had been daydreaming. To do this, dad needs a clock that was near the person who saw the flying."

"That's amazing! How did Dad learn to do this?"

"Each of the husbands and brothers in the family had to learn how to bend time to protect the secret. Your dad learned from reading books that have been handed down through the generations. Since your dad is an engineer, it's been a natural fit for him to tinker and improve the science of time bending. He'll start teaching Gabriel this afternoon."

"Gabriel's going to think I'm a big weirdo." Grace sighed.

"I think your brother is going to be so excited for you and eager to learn how to be a guardian," her mom said, giving her a quick smile and squeezing her knee.

"I hope so. Mom, who was Abuela's guardian?" Grace asked.

But her mom pulled into a spot half a block from the school and didn't answer.

Grace sat quiet for a moment.

"Mom, wait," she whispered. "Do we have to bend Adrian's time too? He's seen me fly—twice. Yesterday in the gym, and today on the field."

"I know, mi amor," her mom said, turning towards Grace. "You should have told me yesterday about Adrian, but children don't have to have their time bent. They usually convince themselves as they get older that what they have seen was just their imagination. We let children who have seen us fly be part of the secret until they grow out of believing. What's important is that anyone who sees you doesn't tell anyone else. There may be people in this world who might want to use us or make us use this magic badly. Do you trust Adrian?"

Grace didn't even have to think about it.

"Oh yes, Mami. I do."

"Good. We all need a friend to share our secrets with," her mom said with a smile.

They watched as teachers got into their cars to drive home. Grace and her mom waited until every last one had left before getting out of their car.

"If we see anybody, remember, you forgot your homework and we came back for it. No one will be too hard on a forgetful student." Her mom winked.

Grace smiled. She was a good student, but a few times they had needed to go back to school after hours for a forgotten folder. Normally they'd race back while the staff was still there and buzz the secretary. But this was no ordinary afternoon.

They circled around the building until they found what they needed. Someone had left a window in the science lab on the first floor open, probably to let out the smell of that day's experiment. Not wanting to chance using their magic at that moment, Grace's mom lifted Grace up to see if anyone was inside.

No one was in sight. Grace's mom squatted under the window and Grace stepped on her knee to climb through the window.

"Just be careful and remember your cover story," she reminded Grace. "I'll stay here and keep an eye out while you get that clock."

Halfway through the window, Grace turned to face her mom. "Mom? Can you get the clock instead? And I'll keep watch?"

"No, m'hija, only the person who was seen flying can get the timepiece. That's how it works," her mom said. **"¡Tú puedes!"**

You can do it!

"OK," Grace said. Then, taking a deep breath, she slid to the lab floor, almost toppling a volcano made of colored sand. She realized she had a lot to learn about this flying business.

7
Flying High

Was she really sneaking into school? Grace was nervous. She never liked to sneak or lie, and her mother never let her get away with anything! The fact that her mom was helping her break rules to get into the school after hours showed how important it was to get that clock.

She tiptoed out of the science lab and down the hallway to the stairwell. So far she hadn't heard or seen anyone. She waited a full minute at the bottom of the stairs before starting up. Trying to quiet her beating heart, she repeated her cover story under her breath as she climbed the stairs.

"I forgot my folder, I forgot my folder, I forgot my folder."

Somewhere between the first and second staircase, she realized that her folder story no longer made sense, since her classroom was on the first floor. But even so, she continued up the stone staircase. When she reached the top, she looked out the exact window Mrs. Lavin had been standing at when she had seen Grace fly.

No wonder Mrs. Lavin hadn't called Grace out of class. It would have been really hard to make out who was on the field from here. But Adrian had stopped cold, and no one could mistake his shaggy bright blonde hair for anyone else.

Grace remembered what she was there for—the clock! She tilted her head way back. It was far above her head, definitely a lot higher than she had remembered.

Last night Grace had learned a lot about flying from her mom. Grace had been shocked at how high she could get just by raising her feet one at a time. But the roof of their back porch was about ten feet tall …this stairwell had to be at least twenty!

What if I fall? Grace worried while looking at the cold hard steps.

She took a deep breath to rid herself of the thought. She considered going back for her mom; this would be easy for her. But she remembered her mom's words from last night, "This is a beautiful gift, Grace, but also a big responsibility.

"I'm scared," she whispered. But she thought back to other times she'd been scared. When she was younger, she'd been afraid of the dark. Her mom had said that it was OK to be scared, even healthy. She had said that fear can keep us safe, and that everyone gets scared.

"Even you, Mom?" Grace had asked.

"Of course! But you shouldn't let fear be the only voice that gets a say in what you do. Sometimes fear keeps us from doing things we want to do or even things we have to do. You can listen to what fear is trying to tell you. But then listen to your heart for the real answer."

I let myself be seen, so I have to get the clock, Grace thought, even though fear made her want to run back down the stairs, out the window, and straight home.

She took one step off the top stair and hovered for a moment.

"I'm scared, but fear won't stop me. I have to do this," Grace said out loud. Then she began climbing imaginary stairs into the air, higher and higher.

Before she knew it, she was within arm's reach of the clock. Grace turned around to get a full view of how high she had flown, when she heard footsteps.

8
Lit!

In a panic, Grace was trying to figure out the best way to drop as fast as she could, when her mom's head came into view two floors down the stairwell.

"Grace! You're SO high!" her mom exclaimed. Grace hovered twenty feet above her.

Grace's heart started beating again, and she returned her mother's big smile. She turned and grabbed the clock off the nail that held it to the wall. She floated down carefully, using her mom's "stepping down" method. Once her feet hit the floor, she ran into her mother's arms.

"**Estoy orgullosa de ti,** Grace."

I'm proud of you

"Thank you, Mom. But you scared me!" Grace mumbled into her mom's chest, still shaking from the scare.

"I'm sorry! I thought you might need my help. But I see you had it all under control. Now let's get that clock back to your dad." They raced down the hall, through the science lab, and climbed out the window.

🦋 🦋 🦋

Back home, Gabriel was in the lab with their dad.

"Hi," Grace said shyly. "Pretty weird stuff, huh?"

Gabriel glanced up from the antique

book he and their dad were studying and smiled at Grace.

"Are you kidding? This is lit! I wish I could fly like you, but this guardian stuff is awesome! I can't wait to see you fly."

Grace smiled back. She had learned from listening to Gabriel speak with his friends that "lit" meant "cool" in middle-school speak. It had been a long time since she and her brother had enjoyed doing something together. She felt proud she could do something that impressed him, and happy he was excited to be a guardian.

Grace gave the clock to her dad. He took one look at it and opened a large closet in the corner that held more clocks than Grace had ever seen.

"This one will do," he said. He handed a clock almost exactly like the one from school to Grace's mom.

Well that explains why my parents are

always buying clocks at thrift stores! Grace thought.

"I'll be right back, honey," Grace's mom told her. "I need to replace the clock in the hallway. You head upstairs and fix yourself a snack. Dad and Gabriel will do their work down here."

"Can I watch? Please?" Grace begged.

With a quick shake of his head that clearly meant, "Go now," Grace knew better than to argue. Her dad was labeling the clock from school "*Grace 2023*."

Gabriel looked up and gave her a wave. "Show me some of your tricks later?"

"Sure," Grace said, and left them to their work. As soon as she closed the secret door to the time lab, the ticking immediately stopped, and Grace was left in silence.

I can't believe all of this! Grace thought. Then she headed upstairs to the kitchen. All the excitement had made her hungry.

9
Promises

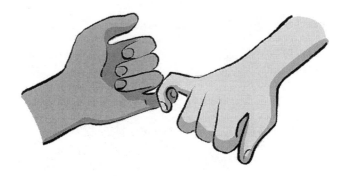

The next day at school, Grace waited to see if Mrs. Lavin would call her out of class but no one came. She and Adrian exchanged a few glances, but despite their nervousness, everything went on like any normal school day.

They finally got to talk at lunch. Grace asked Adrian what Mrs. Lavin had seen.

"She thinks she saw someone fly but she didn't know who it was. I pretended I didn't know what she was talking about."

Grace was grateful. She told Adrian that her dad and Gabriel were "taking care of it."

"Gabriel's in on it? No fair. I guess he is your brother and all. But I'm...practically family! How are they 'taking care of it?'" Adrian wanted all the details.

Grace shook her head. "That part I'm not allowed to tell you."

Grace didn't want Adrian to think her dad was going to do anything to make him "forget" too.

At recess, Adrian asked Grace if she would fly again for him.

"Come on, this time we can go to that corner where NO ONE can see anything, not even from the windows. **¿Por favor?**" Please
he pleaded with hands grasped in front of him.

Grace held strong. She had seen how seriously her parents had reacted about Mrs. Lavin. She knew they did not want to bend time again anytime soon.

"Not a chance! My flying days at school are over," Grace said in a low voice.

Nearby Nolton was watching them from his game of dodgeball. He was still staring at Grace when he cocked his arm and threw a ball hard at a second grader.

"But you'll still teach me, right?" Adrian asked.

She placed her arms on his shoulders. "There's something I need to tell you. It's only women in my family that can fly. I can try to teach you, but…I don't think it will work."

Adrian looked crushed.

Grace gazed intensely into Adrian's eyes. "Adrian, I need to ask you to promise. Promise me you won't tell anyone. You know I'd never ask you to keep a bad secret.

This is a good secret. But even a good secret could become bad…if the wrong people ever found out about my power."

Adrian held Grace's gaze. "I promise. I was so scared yesterday. I was worried Mrs. Lavin knew it was you and that you'd get taken away to someplace awful where they'd keep you and run tests and stuff on you. I'd never want that for you. I promise."

Grace smiled at her friend. "Good. But even without hovering or flying, I can still beat you at tag! You're it!" She tapped his shoulder and dashed off. Adrian tore off after her.

The rest of the day went by quickly. When the bell rang, Grace was relieved to pack up her bag and go home. Whatever it was that her dad and Gabriel had done must have worked.

She was excited to continue her flying lessons with her mom after school.

10
First Flights

After dinner that night, Grace and her mom practiced new flying techniques in their wooded backyard. Grace was surprised to see Gabriel joining her dad to watch.

"Aren't you going to play with your friends?" she asked him.

"Are you kidding me? This is so much cooler!" Gabriel responded.

After Grace's scare in the stairwell, her mom decided to teach her how to do pencil dives from higher heights for when she needed to drop in a hurry.

Soon Grace and her mom were ready for a break. They flew up to a tall branch in the huge oak tree in their backyard. Her dad and Gabriel looked so small below them.

She heard her dad say, "Time to finish up your homework so we can get back to your training." He put his arm around Gabriel and led him back to the house.

Relaxing into the nook of the giant tree, Grace asked her mom about her first flying experiences.

"Will you tell me about when your mom, my abuela, first found out you could fly?" Grace's mom smiled. Grace knew her mom loved talking about Grace's abuela, who had passed away years ago.

"Well, you know your abuela named me

Violet because she loved gardening. We had a small house and a tiny yard, but it was full of blooms. Mrs. Sanchez, our next-door neighbor, lived alone and loved giving Abuela gardening advice, often with a side of homemade pound cake."

Grace interrupted, "Is that the same pound cake recipe we make?"

"It sure is! The best ever. As soon as my mom's car pulled into the driveway, Mrs. Sanchez would poke her head out of her side door. 'Your roses need to be pruned and your hydrangeas aren't getting enough water. And, oh, I made this cake fresh today. Thought you and Violet would like some.'

My poor mom would be standing there with her arms full of grocery bags racing to make us dinner. But she'd always smile sweetly and thank Mrs. Sanchez for the advice and the cake.

When I was nine, I realized my jumps

could turn into low hovers."

"Just like me!" Grace chimed in.

"Yes! Just like you! And just like you, I didn't want to tell my mom. I was scared to add one more thing to your abuela's worries."

Grace knew the feeling. She had been worried to tell her mom about her "gift" too. She also knew her abuela had worked long hours and struggled to raise her mom by herself.

Her mom continued. "One afternoon, I let myself into the house after school as usual. I was practicing in my bedroom and had just gotten to the point where I could jump one, then two, then three feet off the ground. I went out to the backyard to try to jump even higher.

I was so excited by how high I was going that I didn't notice Mrs. Sanchez watching me over the fence from her sunroom. I just caught sight of her large blinking eyes beneath her curly gray perm before I sank to the ground.

I was so scared! I ran into my house wondering how much Mrs. Sanchez had seen and what she'd tell your abuela."

Grace's eyes were wide. "Mom! What did you do?"

"Well, I started pacing, waiting for my mom. When my mom's car pulled into the driveway, I heard the creak of Mrs. Sanchez's side door.

She called out to your abuela, 'Oh! I'm glad I caught you before you ran inside! I was sitting in my sunroom when I saw Violet clear over the fence! You didn't buy her one of those pogo sticks, did you? I hear they are VERY DANGEROUS! She must have been three feet in the air for me to see her head, like a bird above the fence! You really shouldn't let her do that, she'll hurt herself!'"

Grace's mom shook her head. "I mean, I don't think she even took a breath!"

"What did Abuela say?" Grace asked her mom, hanging on every word.

"She was cool as a cucumber. She said, 'Thank you so much, Mrs. Sanchez. I'll certainly have a talk with Violet about this!' and closed the door.

I was so worried what she would think. But Abuela just turned around, gave me the biggest smile, grabbed me into a huge hug, and said, 'Te amo, Violeta.' That was the afternoon Abuela found out about my gift and shared that she too could fly! My training began that night."

Grace's mom explained that she had needed to be extremely careful about flying when she was growing up because they didn't have anyone to act as a time-bender. Grace was curious about what

Grand-father

had happened to her **abuelo**, her mom's father. Her mom once told her that he lived somewhere in Texas.

But while they'd been talking, it had gotten dark. "Time for sleep!" her mom announced, and they both hovered down to the ground.

Soon her mom was tucking Grace into bed. Grace was tired from all the practicing. Her eyes shut even as she asked her mom, "But what happened to Abuelo…"

Her mom kissed her and said, "No more for tonight. Sweet dreams, m'hija."

11
The New Girl

The following week, the school had its annual fall festival with a pumpkin carving contest, scarecrow stuffing, games, and treats set up throughout the parking lot.

As soon as Grace and her family arrived, Gabriel gave a brief wave and ran off to find his friends. Grace and her father visited the attractions while Grace's mother volunteered at the ring toss booth.

They were waiting to take a turn at using a fishing pole to "catch" prizes from a kiddie pool when Mrs. Rings walked up. With her was a girl about Grace's age, with long dark hair and dark brown eyes.

"Grace, this is Mia," Mrs. Rings said. "She's a transfer student and she'll be starting in our class on Monday. I thought you might like to take Mia around the festival and get to know her."

Grace liked the look of Mia. She seemed shy, but her eyes smiled, and when Grace suggested they head over to the moon bounce, Mia nodded her head quickly. "Oh, I love jumping high!"

Grace laughed and said, "That makes two of us!"

The girls ran off, leaving Grace's dad chatting with Mrs. Rings.

Adrian was already in the moon bounce when they climbed inside. It had always been his favorite thing about the festival, and it looked like he'd been at it for hours.

"Mia, this is my friend, Adrian."

Adrian said hello and gave Mia a wave as he bounced higher and higher. Grace was tempted to outdo him, but instead she concentrated very hard to jump normally. There were too many eyes all around, and besides, Mia was watching her closely.

Just then, Nolton crawled into the moon bounce and started slamming into them. When he bumped into Mia, he sneered, "And who are you?"

"Mia," she responded, and Grace chimed in, "She's new."

"Great," he said, rolling his eyes, "another girl. Adrian, are you going to spend all your time with her too?" Nolton laughed meanly. "Why don't you ever hang out with the boys, Adrian? Or do you just like playing with girls and using funny words together?"

"If it means hanging out with cool people who are nice, yes, I prefer hanging out with Grace and Mia than YOU!" Adrian responded.

Grace and Mia laughed. Nolton's face turned a hot shade of pink, and he quickly crawled out of the moon bounce.

"Funny words?" Mia asked.

"Just Spanish," Grace said with a laugh.

"Oh, cool! My parents speak Spanish, and I know a little bit too." Mia said.

"Yeah, we both speak it. You'll have to practice with us. Let's go check out the other booths. **¡Vámonos!**" Grace responded.

Let's go!

"I'll be here bouncing!" Adrian waved goodbye.

"So where did you move from?" Grace asked Mia as they wandered through the aisles of booths.

"San Antonio. We just moved here last week."

"Wow, that must be a big change. Where are you living?"

"My parents bought this place called River Run Farm."

"I love that place!" Grace exclaimed. "We went to an Easter egg hunt there when I was little. There were cows and ducks and goats everywhere. Do you guys farm?"

"No." Mia shook her head. "The last owners took their animals with them. But they did let me keep the outdoor cat that lives on the farm. I named him **Chulo.** My parents don't really like all that farming stuff. They just wanted a really quiet place to live with no neighbors nearby. It's actually...kind of boring."

Cute

"Any brothers or sisters?" Grace asked.

"Nope, just me," Mia responded, sounding sad. "I wish we had more family around. We had to leave my grandfather in San Antonio."

Grace scanned the crowd and pointed out Gabriel, who was playing football with friends. "There's my brother, but he's so into his friends, video games, and sports sometimes I feel like an only child, too. I get what you're saying about more family. It's just the four of us here."

Just then Mia shouted "Mom!" and ran over to a strikingly beautiful woman with long dark hair. She was standing in a small circle of teachers and parents that included Mrs. Lavin.

Grace ran after Mia but froze when she heard Mrs. Lavin say with a laugh, "I could have sworn I saw this little girl flying on the field from out the window! I mean, really flying! But very, very slow. It was so strange."

Did the time bending work? Grace wondered.

"Later that afternoon, I realized I hadn't

had any lunch. I'd just been a bit woozy and was seeing things!" She giggled. "I even called this poor boy out of class and asked him about it. But of course he didn't know anything. I really have to be careful to regulate my blood sugar." She paused to take a bite of her funnel cake, powdered sugar sticking to her lips and chin. "I mean …a girl…flying…how crazy is that?"

Grace slowly exhaled. *It had worked! Mrs. Lavin thought she had imagined me flying!*

The circle of parents and teachers chuckled good-naturedly at the art teacher's story, then moved into smaller groups of conversation. But Mia's mom stayed frozen with a look of shock on her face. Without knowing why, Grace felt a pang of fright seeing her strange reaction.

Mia shook her mom's arm to get her attention. "Mom! I want to introduce you to my new friend…"

But before Mia could introduce her, Grace called out, "Sorry, I need to find my dad," and raced off.

12
Strange Things

Grace found her dad and started pulling his arm towards the parking lot. "Dad, let's go. I want to go home," she panted.

"What's wrong, honey? This is your favorite event of the year! And we haven't even done the cake walk yet."

Grace didn't know how to explain how strange she felt seeing Mia's mom's reaction to Mrs. Lavin's story.

"I'm just really tired and want to go home."

"OK," her dad said slowly, "let's find Mom. I guess Gabriel can stay with his friends and walk home."

Grace's mom was handing a prize to a child when they walked up to her booth.

"Grace wants to go home," her dad said with a shrug.

"Really? So early!"

Grace gave her mom a serious look. "Yes, Mom, I really want to go."

Grace's mom agreed. "OK, let me wrap up here and get someone to take over the booth. I'll find Gabriel and tell him he can walk home when he's ready. Meet you guys at the car."

Just then, Mia and her mom walked up to the booth. Mia's face lit up when she saw Grace.

"Mom! This is Grace, the girl I was telling you about," Mia said.

Mia's mom smiled at Grace and her family and introduced herself. "Hello. I'm Rose and this is Mia. We just moved here, and Mia will be starting school here on Monday."

Grace's mom and Mia's mom held each other's gaze for an extra beat. Then Grace's mom shook her head and smiled. "Sorry… yes…hi! I'm Violet and this is my husband, Leo. Our son Gabriel is…somewhere around here. So nice to meet you!"

"Mia and I were just heading out. Mia's dad is unpacking, and we should probably get back home to help."

"Oh, where are you all living?" Grace's mom asked.

"River Run Farm. Do you know it?"

"Oh yes, how nice! It certainly is a lot of space!" Violet said.

"Yes. We like our space, don't we, Mia?" Rose said, twirling Mia's long hair.

"Well, welcome to the school! Hope to see

you again soon," Grace's mom called after them as they walked away.

Relieved Mia's mom had gone, Grace ran off.

"Hey, I thought we were going home!" her dad called.

"Nope! I'm good now. I'm going to find Adrian."

Grace was happy to find Adrian alone in the moon bounce. She quietly shared what Mrs. Lavin had said to the group of parents and teachers.

"What did they say?" Adrian asked with wide eyes.

"They kind of laughed it off. She said something about low blood sugar and feeling woozy. I think I'm in the clear!" Grace thought back to her dad and Gabriel in the time lab and felt grateful for whatever they did.

But Grace didn't mention Mia's mom's

weird look at hearing the story. She still wasn't sure how to explain how it had made her feel.

"Phew! What a relief! But what Mrs. Lavin said was weird. Do you think that's what your dad meant when he said he'd handle it? How did he make her see things very slowly?" Adrian was puzzled and wanted answers.

But Grace just shrugged her shoulders. "I don't know."

Grace felt guilty not telling Adrian about her father's special ability to bend time, but he already knew one huge secret.
It would have to be enough for now.

13
Adventure Awaits

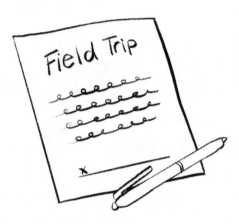

The following Monday, Grace and Adrian helped Mia settle in at school. They introduced her to other kids in the class, but Nolton gave Mia the same sneering smile he had given her in the moon bounce. When it was time for lunch, Grace and Adrian invited Mia to sit with them.

"So why did you guys move here?"

Adrian asked. He crammed a bite of his PBJ into his mouth.

"Gross, Adrian! Ever heard of manners? But yeah, why did you guys come here?" Grace asked. She munched on a neat handful of **platanitos.**

Plaintain chips

"Well, my dad came for his work. So we all had to move. He does something with computers."

Grace laughed. "I'm not very sure what my dad does either. He's an engineer, but I don't know what that actually means."

"My dad works at a bank and takes care of people's piggy banks," Adrian said through a mouthful of peanut butter. The girls laughed. "What! He does!"

When the bell rang for recess, they raced outside for a game of freeze tag. Adrian tagged Grace and left her "frozen" on the far end of the playground. Then Adrian chased Mia off the step of the playset. Mia took a huge jump. No, an enormous jump. And she touched down so slowly.

Grace rubbed her eyes. When she opened them again, Mia had quickly run off with Adrian in pursuit. This secret had her head all screwy. I mean, there was no way their new friend could fly too, right? Back in the classroom, their teacher was passing out permission slips.

"It's very important that everyone brings this back with a parent's signature by the end of this week. The trip to the quarry is next Tuesday, and I'm hoping everyone can join us!"

While they were packing up their backpacks, Mia asked Grace about the trip.

"Yeah, it's supposed to be the best field trip ever!" Grace exclaimed. "I've been excited about this one since kindergarten. We go to this quarry and it's full of water warm enough to swim in! You're going to come, right?"

"Of course," Mia said, but she didn't sound so sure.

🐝🐝🐝

At dismissal, Grace was surprised when Mia lined up for walkers line. "Don't you have to go to the carpool line?

Mia explained, "Your mom mentioned to my mom that kids often play on the playground after school. So she's picking me up in walkers line so we can play together!"

"Cool!" Grace said, although she wasn't sure how she felt about seeing Mia's mom again after her look of shock at Mrs. Lavin's story.

Outside, Grace saw her mom laughing and talking to Mia's mom. The girls ran over to hug their moms. Grace immediately told her mom about the field trip.

"It's next week and you need to sign the

permission form, please!" She handed her mom the paper.

Mia's mom turned to Mia. "A field trip, how fun! Where to, a museum? A park?"

"Actually, it's a quarry with a swimming hole. It's supposed to be really fun," Mia told her.

Grace turned to her mom and said, "There's even a rope swing into the water!"

Mia's mom quickly faced Mia. "Rope swing? Jumping? We'll talk about this at home. Let's go."

"But mom..."Mia started.

"Home. Now," Mia's mom said sternly.

Grace saw Mia's face fall.

"See you tomorrow, ladies!" Mia's mom waved goodbye. She put her arm around Mia, and they walked toward their car.

"I thought we were going to play on the playground," Grace said to her mom.

"I guess they changed their minds."

Grace's mom sounded confused too. Then she called out **'¡Adiós!'** to Mia and her mom.

Goodbye!

To Grace she said, "Did you know they speak Spanish too?"

"Um, yeah, she mentioned that," Grace mumbled, watching Mia open the car door and slump into her seat before they drove off.

14
The Quarry

The day of the field trip was sunny and clear. Grace and her mom walked to school with Grace's bag full of supplies for the day—sunscreen, extra clothes, and her favorite pool towel.

Near the school entrance Mia's mom's car was parked alongside the street. Through the car's open windows, they heard Mia's mom speaking sternly, "Just PLEASE be normal today, Mia. You know what happened last time."

Grace's mom cleared her throat loudly as she and Grace walked past.

"Buenos días," she called out in a cheerful voice.

Good morning

Mia's mom swung around quickly and broke into a nervous smile.

"Oh hi! Buenos días! What a beautiful day for an adventure!"

Grace waited while Mia gathered her things and slammed the car door shut.

"Adiós, mi amor! And remember what we talked about," Mia's mom called to her daughter.

Grace gave her mom a quick kiss, and she and Mia ran to the school entrance. As she turned to wave to her mom, Grace saw that she was still talking to Mia's mom.

"Is everything OK? Your mom sounded really nervous or something," Grace asked. They walked down the hall to their classroom.

"Yeah, she just gets worried sometimes. She really wants me to blend in here. I... I don't really want to talk about it," Mia said quietly.

The classroom buzzed with excitement about the field trip. Kids had their extra bags with swimsuits and flip flops flung over their shoulders, and the teacher could hardly get the class to sit for announcements.

Grace hoped Mia would cheer up on the ride to the quarry.

"I can't wait to spend the whole day together," Adrian said to them as they were lining up for the bus.

Thankfully, the three friends fit on one bench and laughed the entire trip to the quarry.

🪲 🪲 🪲

Today is not a day for flying, Grace thought. She stepped off the bus and smiled nervously at Mia, hoping her new friend couldn't tell what she was thinking. Grace thought Mia still looked a little nervous too. *She must still be thinking about her mom.*

The chaperones separated the children into groups, and Grace and Mia were thrilled to be together. But Adrian shot them a disappointed look when he was grouped with some of the boys in their class, including Nolton.

Grace mouthed, "See you on the bus," as he walked away with the loud group of boys.

Grace and Mia's group found a low edge where they could test the temperature of the water. The cool water felt great on the hot day. It was so clear they could see little fish darting in the sunlight, and Grace and Mia had fun trying to catch them with their hands.

The day was spent swimming and laughing. At lunch, the girls checked in on Adrian, who had his head down and was obviously trying to ignore the rest of his table.

As the girls approached, Nolton was circling the table, choosing his victims to either steal their snacks or make fun of their lunches.

"Adrian, do you think you can sneak off and join our group for the afternoon?" Grace asked.

But just then the boys' chaperone, Nolton's dad, announced, "Lunch is over. Last one to the water is a rotten egg!" He chuckled as his son pushed a boy down in his chair to give himself a head start.

"Ugh," Grace, Mia, and Adrian said in unison.

"I think I have to stick with my group. But save me seat on the ride home. See you later," Adrian said glumly. Then he ran off after the boys.

"I hate that he's having such a bad time," Grace said.

But a few moments later, Adrian was laughing and splashing around with some of the boys. Relieved, Grace and Mia smiled at each other and ran off to catch up with their group.

It was their turn on the rope swing.

15
Free Falling

Grace stood in line for the rope swing, silently repeating to herself, *Don't fly. Just drop. Don't fly. Just drop.*

She couldn't help imagining how everyone would scream if she swung off the rope and accidentally went flying across the water.

Behind her, Mia seemed nervous, too.

"Are you afraid of heights?" Grace asked.

"Not exactly," Mia responded.

The girls smiled at each other and shared a nervous giggle.

"Hope I remember to let go at the right time!" Grace said.

"I was just thinking the same thing!" Mia replied.

When the friendly lifeguard handed Grace the rope, he said, "Don't forget to let go when you swing out!"

With that, Grace stepped off the rock ledge and swung above the water.

"Wooohooo!" she screamed.

She couldn't believe how free she felt. Then she remembered...*Don't fly! Just drop*!

Closing her eyes, she let go of the rope. Her arms clasped tight to her sides, like in the pencil dives her mom had taught her, she fell. Grace hit the cold water with a splash. Swimming up to the surface, she turned to hear her friends on the cliff cheering for her, and Mia gave her a thumbs-up.

I did it! I didn't fly! Relieved and happy, she climbed up to the platform in the middle of the swimming hole.

Now it was Mia's turn. Grace heard the lifeguard give her the same reminder— "Don't forget to let go when you swing out!"—and handed Mia the rope.

Grace saw Mia peer over the edge. It looked like she was shaking a little. Mia stepped off the ledge.

From the platform, Grace thought she heard Mia mumbling something to herself as the rope swung her out over the water. At the moment the rope started to swing back, she let go.

Mia flapped her arms wildly. She looked panicked, but then in an instant, she pulled her arms tight against her body just like Grace had done, and down she went with a splash.

Grace and her classmates cheered as Mia swam up to the surface. She looked relieved to see smiles from her classmates. Mia made her way to the metal ladder of the platform and high-fived Grace.

"I was so nervous," Mia said, shivering and rubbing her arms that were covered in goosebumps.

"You did great!" Grace gave her friend a hug.

Hours of swimming and jumping later, it was time to head home. Kids lined up to walk to the buses. Grace and Mia were swapping favorite moments of their day when Grace stopped. Looking around, she couldn't see Adrian. Where was he?

Nolton's dad was up ahead carrying backpacks to the buses. So why wasn't Adrian with his group? Grace finally spotted him and Nolton on the far side of the quarry.

"Why are they way over there," she said. "Didn't they hear it's time to go?"

Grace and Mia trekked around the huge swimming hole to the base of the rocky hill Adrian and Nolton had climbed. Just as Grace was about to yell up to them that it was time to leave, Grace heard Nolton taunting Adrian.

"I bet you won't, you're too chicken!"

Grace couldn't believe her eyes as her friend walked toward Nolton and a heavy chain that had a large "Danger: No Trespassing" sign.

Adrian glanced back and saw Grace and Mia. Grace waved at him and pointed to the buses across the quarry. Adrian was just about to start down the hill toward the girls when Nolton spotted Grace.

Nolton snorted and yelled, "See! You won't go past the sign, not without your 'girlfriend's' permission!"

Adrian's face turned bright red. He reared back and started running toward Nolton.

Stop!

"Adrian, **¡Para!**" Grace yelled.

But at the last moment Nolton stepped aside, sending Adrian stumbling headfirst under the chain and out of sight.

Grace scrambled up the hill with Mia following behind.

"Nolton!" his dad yelled from across the quarry. "Time to go!"

Nolton pushed past Grace and Mia and ran down the hill and around the quarry toward the buses.

At the top of the hill, Grace and Mia looked over the chain. Where was Adrian?

"Help!" Adrian shouted.

Grace looked down. Adrian was way below them on a small ledge halfway down a cliff with a raging river below.

16
Danger!

"**A**drian! Are you OK?" Grace called to her friend. She and Mia held on tight to the edge of the cliff and peered over.

"It's my ankle. I think I broke it!" Adrian said between sobs.

Grace and Mia looked at each other and then stood to look down the hill and way across the quarry. From where they were

Grace could barely see kids boarding the buses.

"We don't have time, Grace. They're going to leave any minute! What do we do?" Mia asked.

Grace thought out loud, "Mia, stay with Adrian. I'll run back and get help."

But just as Grace peered down to tell Adrian the plan, a piece of the ledge Adrian was on fell into the river below.

Adrian shouted up, "Grace! I'm going to fall any second! Please help me out of here!"

Grace knew what she had to do. Quickly, she calculated the best way to fly down to Adrian and help him get out. Grace decided she would need Adrian to hold on to her hands while she flew him out backwards.

But could she? She had never carried anything heavier than the clock while flying. Would she be strong enough to fly her friend up a twenty-foot cliff wall? Grace knew she had to try. She grabbed Mia by the shoulders.

"Mia, I have to do something. Please promise you'll never, ever tell anyone what you're about to see."

"What? What are you doing?" Mia asked in a frightened voice.

To herself, Grace said the words that she needed to hear. *Fear won't stop me. I have to do this*...She stepped off the cliff.

She was falling so fast! But Grace remembered to put her arms out to slow down, then moved her hands out in front of her like stop signs. She stopped to hover directly above Adrian.

Adrian's face was twisted in pain, but when he looked up at Grace hovering above him his mouth spread into a wide smile.

"You did it! I was hoping you would."

Grace reached for Adrian's hands. He grabbed hers, but when Grace tried to pull Adrian up the cliff...she struggled. He was too heavy. She rose stepping her feet up one at a time, but his weight dragged them down until he was back on the ledge. Grace let go of Adrian's hands and hovered above her friend.

"I can't do it by myself! You're too heavy for me to fly up the cliff."

Adrian's eyes teared up again.

"Try one more time. ¿Por favor?"

Grace nodded. Setting her feet against the side of the cliff above the ledge to give her more stability, she took her friend's hands, pushed off, and began flying up slowly. Adrian helped by pushing himself off the cliff wall with his good foot. But it was no use. Halfway up the cliff, they fell back down again. The ledge quaked when Adrian landed.

"Grace! Grace!" Mia called down.

Leaving Adrian, Grace flew back up to Mia.

"Mia, I'm sorry I couldn't tell you before. I thought I'd be able to get Adrian out this way, but he's too heavy for me." Grace met Mia's awed gaze. "As you can see, I can fly."

Mia smiled.

"It's amazing! Unbelievable, really. Because …well, I can too."

17
Together on Three!

Grace's jaw dropped. Then her mouth closed and turned into a smile.

"Yeah, right! Mia, it's not time to joke! How are we going to save Adrian…"

Mia took a step forward and hovered above the ground in front of her friend.

"You CAN fly!" Grace yelled.

Both girls glanced nervously across

the quarry. The buses were still there but Mrs. Rings and Nolton's dad were talking to Nolton, and he was pointing toward the cliff.

"Yes. I can't believe that you can too." Mia said with tears in her eyes.

"Since you can fly, we can pull him out together!" Grace said. She hovered up.

"Wait! Stop." Mia grabbed Grace's hand to pull her back down. "I...I don't think I can do it. I don't know how to control my flying. Plus my mom said I was never allowed to do it again."

"But we have to help Adrian," Grace said. "My mom has been teaching me and I can show you how, but we have to hurry!" Grace gave Mia a quick flying lesson that covered all the basics.

"OK, to rise up or down, pretend you're climbing stairs. To stop, picture yourself coming to a halt and hold up your hands facing out. To slow down, put your toes up and arms out. Speed up by clasping your arms to your sides and pointing your toes."

Mia mimicked each motion as Grace talked.

"Got it. But I'm scared! What if I fall too? You can't get us both out," she said.

"It's the only way to save Adrian. It's OK to be scared, but don't let fear stop you. Listen to your heart." Grace gave Mia a reassuring squeeze.

Grace and Mia looked down at Adrian. He let out a moan from below.

"Um....guys, can you hurry up? My ankle is turning purple."

More chunks of the ledge fell away into the raging waters below.

"Help!" he yelled up.

Mia nodded at Grace. "I'll do it," she said.

The girls stood side by side and held

hands. "On three!" Grace said. "One, two …three!" and the girls jumped off the cliff. "Toes up! Arms out!" Grace commanded to slow their fall. The girls hovered down to where Adrian was.

"Her too?!" Adrian whispered in awe. "No fair!"

The girls extended their hands to him.

"Now, we need to pull him up hard and use all our flying power to get up this cliff! Pull!" Grace said.

Grace and Mia pulled on Adrian's arms and started their flight back up the cliff.

"Pretend you're stepping up on stairs. Up, up, up," Grace instructed.

"It's working!" Adrian exclaimed when they rose past the halfway point.

"Grace! Mia! Adrian!" One of the teacher's voices rang out across the quarry. "They're coming! Hurry before anyone sees us!" Grace said.

The girls pulled with all of their might. Just as they rose to the top of the cliff, the top of two teachers' heads came into view up the side of the hill from the quarry.

"¡Bájense!" Grace commanded. She and Adrian fell to the ground, but Mia, hovering mid-air, let go of Adrian's hand and froze.

Get down!

"DROP!" Grace commanded again. The teachers were scrambling over the top of the hill. Grace reached up and pulled Mia down hard. Mia's toes touched the ground just as the teachers saw them.

"What is going on here! We've been looking everywhere for you! And why are you past the chain?" Mrs. Rings exclaimed. "Adrian…are you hurt?" Adrian was clutching his swollen ankle.

The three friends looked at each other, exhaled, and broke into huge smiles.

Adrian responded, "Yes, it's my ankle. I think it's broken." But as the two teachers discussed how to get him back to the bus, he turned to his two friends and whispered, "Besides that, everything is awesome!"

Grace peered over the cliff just in time to see the ledge Adrian had just been on crumble and fall away into the river below.

We did it, Grace thought.

18
The Ride Home

Grace and Mia sat together in the back of the mostly empty bus. A lot of their classmates were riding home from the quarry with their parents or carpooling with chaperones.

Adrian was in the front seat with an ice pack on his ankle surrounded by teachers taking turns scolding and fussing over him.

Mia leaned in close to Grace. "So when did you first find out you could fly?"

Grace told Mia how she had started by jumping and hovering on her trampoline.

"Then my mom started teaching me how to fly in our backyard," Grace explained.

"That's so much like how I started. Except my mom had a different reaction."

"What happened?" Grace asked.

"It was about six months ago. I was practicing basketball in the garage of my house in Texas. I was trying to do a slam dunk but couldn't get up to the rim.

So I watched some videos of NBA players and noticed how they stepped up when they jumped. I tried it and it worked! But the weird part was that after I dunked the ball and let go...I didn't fall to the ground! I kind of hovered mid-air. I was shocked. I did it over and over again, and each time, it was the same.

After practicing for a couple of days, I wanted to show my parents. I told them to sit on the stairs in the garage. They were used to watching my magic shows when I was younger, but I was excited for them to see this. Real magic!

I said, 'Mom and Dad, watch this!' and then slammed dunked the ball and let go of the hoop. Then I hovered above the ground and turned to watch their reaction."

"What did they say?" Grace asked.

"My dad started laughing and clapping. I think he must have thought he had a basketball star and magician on his hands.

But my mom's face turned white. She started screaming, 'No! No! No! Get down, Mia! NEVER, NEVER let me see you do that again.' I couldn't understand why she got so mad."

Mia's eyes welled up with tears.

"I asked her, 'Why?' and she said, 'Doing

that is not normal! It will make people call you names. You are never to do that again. Do you understand?'"

Grace remembered the expression on Mia's mom's face when Mrs. Lavin had talked about a girl flying. "Do you know why she said that?

"Not really. She just told me to wish it away hard. I tried. But one day I had this friend over at my house and was dying to show her. My mom walked in just as I started hovering up. I fell down hard and hurt my wrist. People started talking about me at school. My parents decided to move after that."

Grace wrapped her arm around her new friend.

"I'm so sorry. So you never tried again until today?"

"I didn't have anyone to teach me," Mia whispered.

"That must be hard. My abuela taught my mom everything she knows about flying and my mom is teaching me." Grace paused while a thought occurred to her.

"Do you have an abuela?" she asked Mia.

"On my dad's side, but not on my mom's. She was raised alone by my abuelo," Mia responded, looking puzzled.

"It's crazy we can both fly, right?" Grace's eyes went wide. "How old is your mom?"

"Thirty-six. Why?"

"My mom just turned forty, and she only had a mom growing up. Your mom is thirty-six and only has a dad."

"So…" Mia started.

"Our moms could be sisters!" Grace burst out.

Both girls popped their heads over the top of the bus seat to make sure no one was listening to them. But the teachers at the front were still fussing over Adrian so they sank back in their seats.

"That's crazy!" Mia said, smiling and shaking her head. But seeing Grace was serious, her smile faded. "Do you really think we could be family? That would mean we're…"

"Cousins!" they finished together.

When the bus returned to the school, teachers helped Adrian off the bus first. The girls hurried to ask him about his ankle.

"The teachers think it's just a bad sprain. See you tomorrow." As they turned to go, he called out, "And thank you. You guys are awesome!"

"Bye, Adrian!" Mia called back.

"Adiós, Adrian. Feel better." Grace said, giving her friend a smile.

Mia and Grace's mothers were talking to each other in the parking lot. The girls ran to give their moms big hugs.

"Whoa! That's quite a hug, honey!"

Violet said as Grace wrapped her arms around her.

"Mom, Mia and I have A LOT to tell you," Grace said.

"Yes, Mom…we need to fill you in!" Mia said to Rose.

Violet winked at Rose.

"Well, we have some things to share with you girls too. How about everyone comes to our house and we can talk there?"

19
Familia

Family

When they arrived at Grace's house, Grace was surprised to see Mia's dad on the couch, sitting next to her dad and Gabriel.

"Dad! What are you doing here?" Mia asked. Her father looked up at Rose.

"So, girls," Rose started, "we figured out some things today after we dropped you off at school. Violet and I got to talking about where we were from and about our families."

Rose smiled at Violet, and Grace's mom came over and put her arm around Rose.

The girls stared at each other.

"Girls. It turns out...well, it's become clear that..." Rose started.

"You're sisters!" Grace blurted out.

"And we're cousins!" Mia added.

"What? How did you know?" Violet asked. Rose and Violet stared at the girls expectantly.

"Well..." Mia locked eyes with Grace. "Today, our friend Adrian had an accident at the quarry. He fell over a cliff."

"Oh goodness! Is he OK?" Grace's mom asked.

"He hurt his ankle. I think he's going to be fine. But the only way Grace and I could help him was by...flying together."

"What?!" all four parents yelled at once.

"Mia, what did I say about this? Oh my goodness!" Rose started pacing the living room. "Mia, Grace, did anyone see you two fly?"

"No," Grace said. "Well, only Adrian. Flying was the only way to pull him from a ledge on the cliff. It was, kind of, amazing."

"I never could have done it if Grace hadn't taught me how," Mia said.

Rose stopped pacing to face her daughter.

"Mia, that was so dangerous. You could have gotten hurt again. I told you to never …" Her voice trailed off. She sat down hard on the sofa. "And what if we have to move again?"

Grace's heart leapt. She had just found her cousin; she didn't want to lose her so soon!

She asked her aunt, "Why would you have to move?"

"I guess we should fill you girls in. I only remember being raised by my father. Your abuelo, Mia." Mia sat next to her mom on the couch to listen.

Rose continued, "I don't remember my mother and I didn't even know I had a big sister till today. When I showed my dad I could hover when I was about your age, he told me to wish it away, hard."

"You can fly, too, Mom? Oh my gosh! But wait, why did he say that?" Mia asked.

"I didn't understand either and kept asking him. He finally told me that my mom had been able to fly and that she had wanted him to learn strange magic to help her, but he had refused."

"It's called time-bending. It's how we protect our flyers," Grace's dad chimed in.

"Then one day, the town gossip saw my mom fly. She flew to save a child from being hit by a car. But the gossip told everyone

Witch

Breads and cakes

in town that my mom was a **bruja**. My dad said people stopped talking to us and coming to our bakery, even though he made the most delicious **panes and pasteles**. My dad told me he didn't want that for me. So we had to go away. He took me to another town where we didn't know anyone and could start over."

Violet sat on Rose's other side. "I was already six and would have never stopped talking about my mom. So he left me with Abuela. We never stopped looking for Rose."

Rose faced her daughter on the couch. "Since we don't have guardians, we have to move if our secret gets out."

Violet put her hand on Rose's shoulder. "We're sisters and we're going to have to figure this out together. If you and Mia are willing, Grace and I would love to teach you both to fly."

"And Gabriel and I would be honored to teach you the secrets of how we help our flyers stay safe if they are seen," Grace's dad said to Mia's dad.

Mia's parents looked at each other and then at Mia.

"Please?" Mia whispered. She stood and grabbed Grace's hand.

"Yes," Rose finally said. "Yes. It's time for us to stop running, move on from our past, and bring this family together. I want to be with **mi hermana,**" she said, looking at Violet.

My sister

"I'll let you teach Mia. But my father, I mean, our father, made me fear flying too much. It's too late for me," Rose said with tears in her eyes.

Violet turned to her sister. "Our ability to fly is a gift. It's OK to be scared, but fear doesn't have to keep you from doing something you want to do. We'll all learn together, **juntas.**"

Together

115

Rose looked at Mia's pleading eyes, her husband's reassuring smile, and nodded.

"Yes. Our mom saved a child's life, and our girls saved their friend today. I'd like to learn. I will try."

Mia and Grace hugged for what felt like the hundredth time that day.

Cousin

Gabriel wrapped his arms around both girls and said to Mia, "Nice to meet you, **prima.**"

Mia smiled. "I have two cousins! And an aunt and uncle!"

Then the girls both gave a small jump at the same time, pointed their toes, and flew out of Gabriel's arms up to the ceiling— their gift on display for their family to see.

20
New Beginnings

The next day outside the school, Adrian hobbled over to Grace and Mia on crutches. They huddled by the flagpole, away from the rush of kids heading inside. Adrian wore a sideways smile as he looked from Grace to Mia. He shook his head.

"I still can't believe it!"

"Neither can we!" Mia responded.

"How is your ankle?" Grace asked her friend.

"It's just sprained," Adrian said. "I need to wear a brace for a while and use these crutches. It was so dumb of me to try fighting Nolton. Sorry I put you guys in such a bad situation."

"If it weren't for your fall, we wouldn't have figured out that we..." Mia stopped mid-sentence.

"That you're birds of a feather?" Adrian laughed. "Get it, feather...like birds?"

The girls both groaned at his joke.

"Actually, we have more news, but we'll tell you at lunch," Grace whispered.

"I can't wait till then!" Adrian whined. "Besides, I can't even go out to recess since I'll be sitting in detention with Mrs. Lavin because of my little quarry misadventure."

"Rules are rules!" Grace laughed. "But we'll miss you. How long do you have to stay in for recess?"

"Two whole weeks! But that's about the time my ankle brace comes off, so I guess it's not that bad. I just hope she lets me draw instead of making conversation the whole time."

The girls laughed, but then Grace's face became serious. "As long as she doesn't go back to questioning you about your..." She lowered her voice before adding, "flying friend."

"Don't worry. Your secret..." Then he looked at Mia too. "Both of your secrets are safe with me," he whispered.

"We know," Mia said.

"But what's this news?" Adrian asked again.

"OK, OK, I guess we can tell you now, since we still have time before the bell rings." Grace and Mia leaned in close to Adrian.

Grace started, "So we figured out yesterday that we're actually...cousins!"

"What?" Adrian smacked his forehead. "How is that even possible? But now that you say it, I can see the family resemblance, and, well, it does make sense that you can both...you know. That's incredible!"

The girls took turns telling the story they had learned from their moms. How their abuelo had wanted Mia's mom, Rose, to have a "normal" life and took her away before she had memories of her mother and sister. How Rose had been shamed for flying by their abuelo and had never been able to use her gift.

"So the same day that our moms discovered they are sisters, Mia and I figured out we are cousins!" Grace finished.

"Wow!" Adrian shook his head. "That's a lot." He lowered his voice. "So are you guys going to start...flying together? Without me?"

"Well, since you're already in on the

secret, you're welcome to come over anytime to watch our flying lessons," Grace said.

"Flying lessons?" Adrian's eyes widened.

"Yes, my **Tía** Violet is going to teach me, Grace, AND my mom!" Mia said.

Aunt

"Amazing! I'll be there," Adrian said just as the bell rang.

They were so wrapped up in their conversation they didn't see Nolton approaching.

"Hey Adrian! You were slow before, now you're going to watch turtles pass you, Dude!"

But Nolton's face changed from his usual smirk when he looked down at Adrian's ankle.

"I'm actually really sorry about teasing you. I...shouldn't have done that." His voice dropped to a whisper. "Sorry you got hurt so badly."

Adrian smiled at Nolton. "You didn't

make me do anything. I shouldn't have charged at you. But thanks. I'll be better soon. And don't worry, I didn't tell the teachers anything about why I ended up past the sign."

"Thanks, Dude. That's actually really... cool." Nolton quickly scurried away without looking back.

Grace and Mia's mouths dropped open.

"Did Nolton just...apologize?" Grace asked.

"Well, that was unexpected!" Adrian said. He headed toward the entrance. Then he stopped and whirled his head around. "One last question. Where is your abuelo now? The one who took Mia's mom away?"

Grace and Mia turned to each other.

"I mean, if he went through all that trouble to keep your moms apart, what would he think about all of you...you know ...flying together now?!"

The late bell rang, and Adrian turned to hobble into the building on his crutches. Grace and Mia stared at each other.

"What do you think? You're the one who knows him," Grace said.

"My abuelo is nice. I mean, OUR abuelo is nice...I'm sure he'll be great with everything," Mia said, but her voice sounded less than sure. "I guess we'll see when he comes to visit us from Texas next summer."

There were many more questions they'd have to get answers to. But one thing was clear. They were in this...together.

GLOSSARY

abuela (ah-**bweh**-la): grandmother

abuelo (ah-**bweh**-loh): grandfather

adiós (ah-**dyohs**): goodbye

antepasados (ahn-the-pah-**sah**-dos): ancestors

ayúdala (ah-**yoo**-dah-la): Help her

bájense (bah-**hehn**-se): Get down

bruja (**broo**-hah): witch

buenos días (**bweh**-nohs **dee**-ahs): good morning

chulo (**choo**-loh): cute

Dios mío (dyohs **mee**-oh): My God

empanada (em-pah-**nah**-dah): baked or fried
dough filled with meat, veggies, or fruit

enséñame (ehn-she-**nyah**-me): show me

estoy orgullosa de ti (ehs-**toy** ohr-goo-**yoh**-sah-
deh tee): I'm proud of you
familia (fah-**mee**-lyah): family

Guatemala (gwah-teh-mah-lah): Central American country, south of Mexico

juntas (**hoon**-tas): together

mi hermana (mee her-**mah**-nah): my sister

m'hija (**mee**-hah): short form for "my daughter"

mi amor (mee ah-**mohr**): my love

mochila (moh-**chee**-lah): knapsack or backpack

panes y pasteles (pahn-es ee pahs-**tehl**-es): breads and cakes

para (pah-**rah**): stop

platanitos (plah-**tah**-nee-tos): plantain chips

por favor (pohr fah-**bohr**): please

prima (**pree**-mah): cousin

puedo tratar (**pweh**-doh trah-**tahr**): I can try

rápido (**rrah**-pee-doh): fast

te amo (teh **ah**-moh): I love you

tía (**tee**-ah): aunt

tranquila (trahng-**kee**-lah): relax

tú puedes (too **pweh**-dehs): You can do it

vámonos (**bah**-moh-nohs): Let's go

volando (boh-**lahn**-doh): flying

yerba mate (**yehr**-bah **mah**-teh): a bitter tea
   popular in South America

AUTHOR'S NOTE

The idea for this book started as a bedtime story for my daughter, Sophia. It was inspired by a dream I'd had where my mom showed me how to fly. From the very first line, Sophia co-created the characters and the story with me, and then, once she fell asleep, I'd race to the computer to capture it on the page. Written during the pandemic, *The Adventures of Amazing Grace* gave us wings to fly out of our house into a world of magic and possibilities. A place where we could face our fears together and soar.

Sophia and I frequently read together, taking turns on pages or chapters. With that in mind, it is my hope that both children and adults will enjoy getting to know Grace, Mia, Adrian, and their families and that you will share this story with someone you love. To make this book more accessible for all kinds of readers, it was printed in a dyslexia-friendly font.

If you enjoyed this book, please leave a review on Amazon or Goodreads. To stay updated on my latest projects, follow me on Instagram or visit **www.erikaferrarilopez.com.**

It was exciting, and honestly, a little scary to write my first book. Thank you for reading it! And if fear is stopping you from doing something you love, remember what Grace would say, "Fear can't stop you. You can do this!"

ACKNOWLEDGEMENTS

First and foremost, my gratitude to our Lord, who makes all things possible.

To my motivator, coach, writing partner, editor, and the inspiration for Grace, my daughter, Sophia. Thank you for creating this book with me and gently, and not so gently, nudging me toward its completion and publication. You made this happen!

To my husband, Len, who always encourages me to pursue my dreams, and to my son, Christian, whose gentle soul, humor, and big heartedness inspire me every day.

To my Mami who came to me in a dream and taught me to fly, you are still inspiring me, even from heaven. To my family and friends, especially my kitchen cabinet—Kirsten, Meredith, and Renata—for having my back in all things—I love you. Thank you to Kathy

Izard, whose mentorship and coaching taught me to trust the whisper and take my writing seriously. To my Wordplay group members who have encouraged my writing and helped shape this book with their brilliant insights and to our brave, caring leader, Maureen Ryan Griffin, the midwife of our stories! To my editor Catherine Nichols, illustrator Amber Orozco, and designer Sheila Smallwood— thank you for bringing Grace to life! Muchas gracias to Indhira Caceres for double checking the Spanish used in the book.

And finally, to my AMAZING beta readers, Alice and Olivia Komers, Allie Dryburgh, Anna Ficke, Anne and Miriam Fox, Eleanor Sloan, Emma Caceres, Evie Pirrone, Gabi Bittner, James and John Fatzinger, and Nora Foy, who read *The Adventures of Amazing Grace* in multiple forms, thank you for your suggestions, for your feedback, and especially for your excitement and love of Grace!

Erika Ferrari Lopez lives in Charlotte, North Carolina, with her wonderful husband, two marvelous children, and two adorable and sometimes naughty dogs. She grew up in northern Virginia as a daughter of two Latin American immigrants and spent summers running through coffee fields in Guatemala. Erika began writing memoir and essays in 2017. *The Adventures of Amazing Grace* is her first children's book.

Made in the USA
Columbia, SC
20 November 2023

26550415R00083